11th July 08

A Summer Talent

by

R. J. Neale

authorHOUSE®

AuthorHouse™ UK Ltd.
500 Avebury Boulevard
Central Milton Keynes, MK9 2BE
www.authorhouse.co.uk
Phone: 08001974150

First published by AuthorHouse   3/18/2008

ISBN: 978-1-4343-7680-0 (sc)
ISBN: 978-1-4343-7679-4 (hc)

Printed in the United States of America
Bloomington, Indiana

This book is printed on acid-free paper.

Front cover by kind permission of © Bryan Eveleigh, copyright reserved.   Contact: bryan@beimages.co.uk

The author is indebted to Margaret, Bryan and Caroline for their valuable help.

Dedicated to Mum & Dad

Chapter One

The Arrival

April had just begun, the sweet smell of spring hanging in an unbroken blue sky; without a doubt summer was just about to bloom. The wild life that surrounded me was breathtaking to behold, with its wondrous purity that had always eluded the comprehension of Man. A truly wonderful equinox had arrived but, by the time May was upon us, the heat had become almost unbearable.

Sessile Standmore and his new wife Linda Lillycrap had become the newest additions to the small community we called home. Set in some of the most beautiful countryside within the county, nestling amongst deep, lush green valleys, slept our small village known as Well-Bottled. To enter this idyllic village there is only one route available - to take the left hand turning at the crossroads at the top of the third and largest valley that had for so long shrouded the area in secrets never disclosed until now. The road, aptly named Laid Out Lane, was a long, twisting, narrow path which carried the traveller to the very heart of this most tranquil setting, finally reaching the highly desirable village of Well-Bottled.

The local Police Constable, a recent newcomer to the location himself, had settled in rather well. (Unofficial title - christian name "Paul", surname "Ovary" - thus meaning the new village law enforcer is, in fact, PC Paul Ovary - one of life's strange ironies, yet many more were to become unravelled as time went by).

Paul was one of the first amongst the villagers to have met Sessile and Linda, only knowing this due to the unavoidable sound of laughter coming from the green located at the centre of the village which I overlooked - as did the Pub, The Pieced and Broke Arms - which in turn I could see clearly from the master bedroom of the property that had been entrusted to me by my parents following their decision to move some eight years earlier to a village quite some distance away from the unfolding events that you are about to be told. So, the house that I grew up in at long last became mine, being the only child - or so I thought at the time.

Towards the north end of the green stood Clive the Cobbler, who had lived in the village for as long as I could remember, having had his business passed down to him from his father, and his father before that. The shop was very quaint and had a most charming air

3

about it. Unfortunately for Clive, owing to the most revolting eating habit imaginable - a strategically placed, heaped spoonful of food would be thrust into the anticipating mouth every fifth second or so, while his head would be poised at a truly remarkable forty five degree angle prior to the eventual demise of the substance yet to be consumed - the most dreadful nickname Gobbler the Cobbler had crept into use over the years. Clive had become more or less part of the furniture at The Pieced and Broke Arms, having fallen deeply in love with the landlady, a sprightly young thirty-something blonde, whose partner had run off with the postman seven months after they had taken over as the new landlords. Although this was most unfortunate, if only because of the loyalty shown by Miss Ploughman to Peter the Postie - who had seemed the epitome of a dashing young character of old but had turned out to be nothing more than a scallywag of the highest order - the strong natured and disciplined Miss Ploughman had built a very sturdy rapport with the locals (of which I am now led to believe there were more than seventy) who, I must say, found her company an absolute delight.

Looking westerly there was an unquestionable air of unease. From my peripheral vision I could just about make out the silhouette of Mrs Bircher, the retired Governess of the Girls' Convent School, just slightly behind her net curtains that were washed on a very regular basis but seldom down for any longer than a few moments, despite which her presence was just visible on most days.

The Reverend Dr Bircher, a much admired and respected man, had passed away only two months before, owing to a long period of ill health after taking the School to an island far beyond the reaches of the Southern Hemisphere. On this particular occasion the trip was meant to last no longer than four weeks, but the journey home commenced some six years later with an additional forty pupils. No explanation was ever given, but many still say that's what probably killed him . . . . it is left for us merely to speculate and ponder.

Mrs Bircher wished to retain her marital status after this sullied event, undeniably holding strong beliefs in what is correct. (Even allowing outsiders within the village would be frowned upon unless provisional acceptance had been bestowed by the aforementioned lady's politely spoken but nonetheless point-blank enquiry, "Are they from good stock?" - which meant they were expected to have traced their heritage as far back as possible, and certainly no later than the Crusades).

Facing south was a completely different story. The aged and weathered Vicarage stood proud amid exemplary grounds, cared for by an outstanding gardening company that we will come to a little later. The Vicarage was originally constructed sometime during the latter years of the Sixteenth Century, and I admired it regularly from my rear garden on these stiflingly hot mornings that we had yet to become accustomed to. A far-reaching, translucent shadow would be cast from the exquisite stained glass window of the adjacent Church and, on such mornings as these, what little sense the world made was at best bewildering.

In the distance I could clearly see Major Shoreshot and Lady Belling, an extremely well educated and manicured couple who had run the Church Upkeep Programme since the unfortunate demise of Dr Bircher and now had their permanent residence in The Vicarage, both having completely different and independent interests. Lady Belling could quite easily spend hours on her most favoured interest, this being campanology - another of life's strange ironies! - while the Major, an ex-military man, seemed to have relinquished the wish ever to hold a firearm again and had decided to take up the more genteel pastime of archery. However, in doing so he became more than a little eccentric in appearance - in fact, he looked absolutely ridiculous dressed permanently in green.

The Major had one child from a previous marriage but unfortunately, owing to the antics he would get up to with his military chums, there was little doubt that the years he had spent with Beatrice were nothing more than a miserable sham. The only compassion he had shown was during Beatrice's difficult pregnancy but, despite this, a dark cloud still hung over their relationship.

Beatrice, after a full term plus three weeks, gave birth to the son the Major longed for. Nigel, a healthy eight pound baby boy, had come into the world after putting his mother through twenty nine hours of labour and excruciating pain. Nigel's presence offered some relief to the tense situation following the short happy period of his birth but, forever entertaining and being strong in many social circles, his parents found it most difficult to conceal their antagonism and, while falsely joyful faces would be presented by both parties at social gatherings, other guests were perfectly sensitive to the situation and a knowing silence had become almost deafening at such events.

Once a month a property owned by Lady Belling would be used for early evening dining followed by croquet on an evergreen lawn that had yet to be seen with a blade of grass out of place. Beatrice, meanwhile, had formed a very close friendship with the only remaining member of staff that Lady Belling employed - although at one time the Belling family had carried forty or so staff, over the years this had diminished to just one, the most loyal. Strange in appearance, at a height of four foot two and with a voice suggestive of someone having inhaled an air balloon full of helium, this is the man with whom Beatrice would be unfaithful to her husband - Sydney. As for Nigel, he hardly ever spoke about his mother for Lady Belling had, in truth, brought up the young child from an extremely early age as if he were her own - which to all intents and purposes he really was.

Sydney, being of West Indian origin and appearing not to have any other history but for his employment with Lady Belling, vanished mysteriously, as did Beatrice, possibly both heading in a westerly direction.

All that remained in Sydney's apartment on closer inspection were some banana skins, one single apple core, three cans of dried tomatoes, a boomerang, six masterly crafted pipes, a limbo dancing stick still erected ready for use, and a small pouch of tobacco; and finally, the only thing left for me to report on this most distasteful of events is that there was always an unusual smell emanating from that apartment.

Now at the summer of his years, Nigel - not ever finding love again after being jilted at the altar by his childhood sweetheart Samantha some eleven years ago - found himself not wanting even to try. "Love is for losers", he could be heard to say repeatedly, in the corner of The Pieced and Broke Arms after his customary half a shandy extra light that always made him feel the cogs were well lubricated. Not particularly a big drinker, he would tend to light a cigar with his second half, the cigars being supplied to him free of charge by his aviation pals. Nigel had unexpectedly passed the exams to become the Navigation Officer at the nearby airfield - actually he was also ground crew, co-pilot, steward , and indeed also ran the cafeteria. Consequently, the majority of these cigars would have come from a south westerly bearing and, looking as if he had a civil war cannon placed in his mouth, it became increasingly challenging to see across the bar.

Nigel was only supposed to be at Well-Bottled for a short duration, having suffered an attack of the illness that had troubled him from the day he was jilted, Knocking Knee Syndrome - the result of a strict upbringing by his father the Major, who only allowed him to join the model making club on his twenty third birthday, simply to discover that Nigel had been elected Secretary of the Model Makers Society and entrusted with all duties - a most enviable position to have held. However, a cruel twist of fate left him in hospital after an altercation at the year-end Model Makers Dinner and Dance, involving some extremely strong glue, a magnifying glass, and a particularly sharp plastic cutting tool. This, therefore, was the end of Nigel's sanctuary. It must be said that the limp and the most frightful halitosis imaginable did not help - either way he had been through a rough time of late.

Dr Stillwell kept a very close eye on the goings-on around the village - rarely seen or heard, but always attentive. The Surgery - about the size of a large cupboard - was at the east end of the green, where the sun shone during the morning, just the way the Doctor liked it. Patients entering the Surgery would, as a rule, trip on the shallow step just beyond the reception desk - which the Doctor found most amusing? Nancy the Nurse was trusted implicitly by Dr Stillwell, clearly having an air of majesty about her person - a creation of womanhood in perfection - she really was quite something.

Nigel had been referred to a number of specialists on numerous occasions after such a spell of his illness but, every time an appointment was made on his behalf, Nancy would be on call - almost never in the surgery. Fortuitously in this instance she was on the premises, in the dispensary concocting a new formula of sun protection. Today, in the twentieth day of temperatures in excess of one hundred and ten degrees Fahrenheit, their paths had yet to cross. Could this vision of beauty be the answer to Nigel's troubles?

Where will these out of the ordinary happenings lead us? Why did Linda Lillycrap look so surprised all the time - something to do with the botox injection perhaps? Will

Miss Ploughman eventually fall for Clive's affections? And who did look after Lady Belling's grounds so impeccably? To these questions yet unanswered, continue to read this nonsense and discover the truth that lies beneath the perplexity of escapades yet to be revealed.

Chapter Two

The Acquaintance

Some weeks had passed since the refit of The Pieced and Broke Arms, to the absolute joy of anyone who frequented this particular watering hole on a regular basis. The Pub had been in a bad state of repair for some time owing to a lack of ambition on the part of the former landlord. However, the shrewd business plan devised by Miss Ploughman - to form a Committee for the most regular of users to grow their own hops, and register this under the umbrella name of the Pieced and Broke Arms *issers - became an outstanding success, with the help of an entrepreneurial acquaintance who had the power to launch a huge publicity campaign - more or less on an international scale - which led to an overwhelming response.

Major Shoreshot had a vested interest in the above - no doubt somehow connected with his nomination as Committee Chairman after forwarding a substantial figure of funds for the venture - and felt most assured by the experience, together with guidance proffered by Gregory, who was known also to Miss Ploughman from her years spent at University.

Sessile and Linda were both still waiting for the Reopening date to be announced. Not having indulged themselves in this particular undertaking, they seemed to have quite a keen interest in the frivolities and electrifying air of excitement that engulfed the village. In spite of this, another week had come to an end and still no-one had been told what night the

Grand Opening would take place. By this time, each Trustee was becoming increasingly more anxious, having invested a large sum of money into the enterprise.

Entering the Pub from one of the fire escapes which had not been closed properly and which, as a result, offered direct access - and confident for sure in the strength of their numbers - a multitude of Committee members entered the refurbished but not quite yet finished building without invitation. "Let me provide you all with a little more understanding of this situation", Miss Ploughman said, in a very composed manner - she was on fire! - definitely not a lady one would dream of opposing.

Unfortunately Nigel, who had been standing behind this particular escape route totally unprepared for the door to be forced open with such voracity and lightning speed, shot off into a state of shock, performing some sort of propelled dance routine which truly had to be seen to be believed . . . . . nothing of which at any point was noticed by one Committee member or angry Trustee. Nigel, who had been given the opportunity by Miss Ploughman to choose the final seating configuration in the restaurant - which he had done creatively, achieving a romantic ambiance even when it was empty - and who justifiably was feeling very proud of his final presentation, ready and awaiting final approval from Miss Ploughman, was now thrown into a state of mental turmoil.

"Would you all like to stop punching the air?" Miss Ploughman said. "I will tell you exactly why we have yet to open!" she added in a very sturdy tone of voice. "The fire escape that you all decided to barge through has been installed the wrong way round and, had you taken the time to look, you would have noticed that the second and third fire exit doors open from the inside out, not from the outside in, and the Major and I are waiting for this problem to be resolved. When, and only when, this dilemma has been corrected, we might just finally obtain the certificate from the Health and Safety Department that we require to resume trading!"

"This outburst has now given me the opportunity to resolve some of the misgivings that you all seem so eager to give voice to. In your mail tomorrow, you will receive a new Shareholders Certificate, and also an advice of the amount of money each and every one of you will receive, according to the share that you hold, and the profit within that. You may also be interested to hear, since you cannot hold your fire, that enclosed with the accounts you will find a letter informing you that Gregory is on the point of expanding the distillery due to the escalating demand for the commodities we are now producing."

"Where is Nigel?" Miss Ploughman asked in a peremptory though nonetheless worried tone. Nigel, by this time, had rocketed himself a number of metres from where he had first stood - having had absolutely no control over the situation and finding his legs moving in a manner closely matching the wings of a humming bird - to the newly installed money making and dispensing machine, where he hovered entwined in the midst of flashing lights and a likeable tune from a musical source.

"What on earth are you doing?" the Major said, as he came through the front door of the Pub, being a keyholder throughout this interim refit period. P.C. Paul Ovary was strolling across the green after finishing his shift, only to hear the commotion emanating from the Pub, and arrived just a few moments before the Major - having eye-witnessed the speed, time and distance covered by Nigel who, according to his exact calculation, was travelling at between thirty three and thirty nine miles per hour! ... "Just try to settle down, everyone", Paul said, "and let us all regain some sort of composure."

At the same time he was trying to gain some stability to Nigel's legs, which still appeared to be locked in some sort of hyperdrive. This was turning out to be an interesting afternoon. Major Shoreshot was now in denial of his son's behaviour, which had led to a situation that was becoming increasingly more difficult to tackle. Nigel, again, was not at fault . . . .

Clive, by this time, was sitting on his favoured bar stool which carried a slight curvature but a most comfortable sitting position, without doubt owing to the amount of time he had spent on it and his continual longing that, unfortunately, passed unnoticed by Miss Ploughman. Clive was not aware that his lost heart would find another, and eventual fulfilment of the love he so longed to give would become a reality - once again through one of those strange ironies that seem to arise throughout this story.

Meanwhile, Gregory had travelled the length and breadth of the country, promoting the new range of beers shortly to be released, including among others such gems as Puddle of Piddle, Holding the Fiddle, Pain in the Brain and, finally, the one closest to Nigel's heart, The Squirrel's Nuts, which had a most uncanny, earthy, woody taste. This had been consumed by Nigel just prior to the forcible opening of the fire exit door .... and may have contributed to the most peculiar behaviour exhibited to all and sundry within the Pub? The truth was, in fact, that Nigel had only just opened the bottle and had sipped less than a mouthful.... Once again, Nigel would be the one to blame.

Gregory had not only successfully won a contract to export the new range of beers to the Continent, but had also broken the hold on the western market. This meant that the anticipated boost in sales was now imminent, attributed not least to his soft, smooth-as-silk voice, the smell of a cologne that somehow put one at ease and a fashion sense which made one feel unworthy to be within twelve paces of his presence. This man was so cool that, if he suffered with dandruff, he would shed snow; and if one had sufficient courage to get close to him - for without doubt ice burns - one could not help but succumb to his powerful aura. He was undoubtedly the best in his profession - a marketing genius the likes of which I had never seen before.

P.C. Paul Ovary had now put Nigel in the recovery position along the outer side of the bar. Never one to complain, with discomfort written across his face, Nigel was in a state of shock. Thus far Paul had made the decision to use the phone in the Pub, never taking his personal phone anywhere with him whilst on duty because it was the only time he could get some sort of peace and quiet. However, on this very evening of all evenings, it was sorely missed.

"Yes, he is", Paul said, as Nigel now lay in agony, just able to overhear what Paul was saying. "Well, send Nancy ... really we need some assistance here! Nigel is just about to go under ... Yes, but make it sharp?" These words were becoming more and more faint to Nigel; his hearing was becoming more impaired with each and every word spoken by Paul.

"Nigel ... Nigel ... Can you hear me ... ?" It had only taken twenty three minutes for Nancy to bring Nigel round from the dysfunctional state in which she had found him.

"There .. there ... there .... is the glue!" were the first words Nigel spoke as he began to regain some sort of consciousness, although not yet able to open his eyes. Nancy had put two freshly washed towels under Nigel's head from the moment of her arrival, and had remained with him throughout his recuperation period. In the execution of these kindnesses, the perfume she wore had impregnated the towels, its seductive bouquet doubtless helping in no small measure to bring Nigel back to a higher level of awareness.

Nancy had left her parents and only sibling at the dining table, unselfishly and typically unfazed about the hours of preparation she had put into the beautifully presented cuisine and the care she had taken to maintain the perfect temperature for its consumption. However, owing to the fog-bound airfield, there had been a long delay. Eventually, take-off had commenced some three hours later than scheduled and Nancy had been waiting patiently for the arrival of her parents and sister but, again, that was Nancy - considerate and understanding - a magnificence of exquisiteness without qualm.

Her father was not a risk-taker, particularly having just purchased his new twin prop, light-winged, full rudder-controlled aircraft in colours not dissimilar to those used during a war campaign. He was a retired pilot from a worldwide aviation organisation, which he had enjoyed so much throughout his working life, and had finally become a director of the company before retiring in his fortieth year of service, having received the commemorative

Golden Flying Duck - the highest of accolades ever awarded in the history of the Quackers Club.

Tiberius and Isabella, and their youngest daughter Tahlia, gave little thought as to where Nancy may have gone, knowing that she would always consider others before herself, thus giving them the opportunity to make themselves more than comfortable. Tiberius now sat, with a loosened tie just held together by the Flying Duck tie retainer which he had received at the fairy tale ball marking the eve of his retirement, which had been accompanied within the presentation box with a companion set of Duck Bill cufflinks which he wore with the utmost pride on any occasion deemed remotely suitable or necessary. Isabella, on the other hand, was dressed ready for bed, although she had decided to keep on her person a brooch given to her on behalf of the Lady Fledglings - a golden egg with a partially cracked shell which carried a slightly exposed duck's head. Tahlia did much the same, and wore her duck feet slippers which, unfortunately, were rather too big and both for the left foot owing to a manufacturing fault. That said, her virtually translucent pastel pink negligee, divine figure and adorable face more than compensated for the craziest of cumbersome walks she had to endure each time the slippers sat upon her feet.

As Nigel opened one eye, shortly followed by the other, . . . "I have died and gone to Heaven, and it's more beautiful than I could ever have imagined," he thought to himself. In truth, he had finally seen the rest of his life in the shape of the angel who had taken the time to look after his battered pride and body . . . Nancy.

Was Lady Belling amongst the Committee members in the Pub? Will we in due course find the truth about the gardening company that continues to keep her grounds so grand? And Clive still awaits the opportunity to give his heart .... for in love he is, but with whom?

Chapter Three

Evergreen

June signalled its ebb tide with a gruelling intensity of heat that was more exhausting and harder to tolerate than anything that had come before. Trees that had once towered evergreen now stood bare, bowed to the inexorable force and supremacy of the southerly wind and falling victim to its hungry scorching heat. Many, in fact, had given way already - destroyed by the essential ingredient craved by vegetation, the sun, which had shone ferociously throughout a flaming June. Born of this - as if punishment to date were not enough - came a sweltering July, and little comfort was taken that of course rain would eventually come, for no-one could tell and, more to the point, no-one would dare venture a guess .... a wise stance to take, for the first day of July had produced an astonishing temperature of one hundred and twenty three degrees Fahrenheit!

Linda Lillycrap had been approached by Gregory because she and Sessile had a water source which lay at the end of their back garden - a well half full of fresh spring water replenished naturally from the largest of the three valleys. Gregory had spoken with Linda on the Thursday of the week before, to arrange a meeting with both her and Sessile to discuss a proposal for the use of this water that was now so desperately needed for the hops as they became more and more parched with each passing hour. These negotiations seemed to have fallen into place satisfactorily for all parties concerned -

how Gregory managed to pull it off remained a mystery to everyone but, of course, that was the very thing that made him the true master of his profession. This was a man with a rare blend of sincere integrity and considerable entrepreneurial skills - whose sense of precision and timing was to die for - so that the final delivery of his masterpiece became more of a perfectly polished performance to a breathless audience than a business plan for consideration by ordinary mortals!

Lady Belling had spent the last few days grooming the treasured and perfectly unblemished garden that surrounded her private cottage, which was set in a hamlet not so far from Well Bottled blessed with the most ridiculous of names - Pigsmellwell. This tiny place really was in the depth of a countryside rarely encountered by the outside world - and it was to this place that Lady Belling repaired infrequently to make peace with herself at times when it seemed necessary to reflect and gather her thoughts. On this most peaceful of occasions she sat on her favourite of all resting places - a three seater wooden bench positioned in the lee of a north-facing wall and shrouded in the shadow it cast. Now, in these tranquil protected surroundings, she would set about trying to relive and understand the episode that had taken place recently in The Pieced and Broke Arms.

Lady Belling had indeed been aware of the events that had unfolded in the Pub, having spent most of the day supervising the installation of a brand new kitchen commissioned by the committee. She had spent hours of her precious little free time cleaning the apparatus that had arrived vacuum-packed, wrapped, housed and hermetically sealed in large packages that took for ever to unpack - which would only finally be used when the Hygiene Supervisor was content that all requirements of the Health and Safety Department for whom she worked were properly met.

This had become a long drawn out process for Lady Belling but, on completing the tiresome task, she had witnessed Nigel being reassured and revived by Nancy, and that split second revelation convinced her that the love Nigel craved so desperately was in fact directly in front of him, for she had witnessed the peace in his eyes as they slowly opened. She had also witnessed the vision of beauty that knelt before him, her prayers answered in the most unlikely of places - The Pieced and Broke Arms. Lady Belling had experienced a rare moment of clarity - indeed the only such moment in a considerable number of years - a welcome and well-deserved alternative moment in a life filled mostly with anxiety.

Mrs Bircher was just approaching the front door of the cottage as Lady Belling turned the corner from her meditations, beating a hasty retreat to the porch where a jug of liquid refreshment - now at a refreshingly icy temperature ready for serving - had been set on a frosted tray that, moments before, had sat in the deepfreeze. Lady Belling - who had recovered to some extent from the oppressive heat, although the shady area had not been cool enough to tame her own body temperature - felt the pick-me-up drink she had made would be something of a shot in the arm!

"Good morning!" she said.

"And a good morning to you," replied Mrs Bircher.

"All ready then?"

"Yes ... are you?"

"Yes … plug it in and we'll be set … the lead is just behind the door," said Lady Belling.

"Okay … all done … can you turn it up?" shouted Mrs Bircher through the door. "Well? … Is it working?"

"Yes … the wireless is working just fine," Lady Belling replied. "Loud enough?"

"Yes, perfect," answered Mrs Bircher.

Every third week during the summer months an arrangement had been made to meet at this particular cottage - possibly because Lady Belling would be sure not to be disturbed owing to the fact that only a handful of close friends knew of its most peaceful existence. Mrs Bircher was one such, and had spent six weeks there after the sad loss of Dr Bircher.

The cottage was not used for more than a few weeks a year, and had been in the Belling family for a number of years. Lady Belling thought it the most valued jewel in her crown - a property portfolio whose size had increased beyond recognition since her father departed this mortal life shortly after her twenty second birthday. However, Lady Belling was an astute and wise young lady even at that tender age, having had one of the best educations the country could provide.

The wireless that the ladies were so eager to get back in working order had received a soaking from a summer's night the year before, having been left outside when the heavens opened and torrential rain fell. Now it was repaired and once again fully operational, and they tuned in to a broadcast that had run from the first week of April through to the last week of September - a nightly show that started at seven o'clock each evening from Monday to Friday, with the omnibus edition on each and every third Sunday afternoon of the month. Lady Belling and Mrs Bircher would get together on these dates because the programme was dedicated to gardening, and both ladies were keener than ever to learn more about this pastime they enjoyed with so much passion.

Although a different presenter would take to the microphone each year, this year was very special because two brothers would be presenting the show - Douglas and Howard Pratt - the Brothers Pratt - a wonderful pair of old-timers from yesteryear. They had taken care and considerable time in choosing a fitting title for their forthcoming wireless broadcasts for the summer season, but their ultimate choice following weeks of agonizing - Don't Squeeze my Plums - although probably well within the spirit of the subject matter, was perhaps not the most fitting at all in the wider sense of the words. Mind you, what they did not know about 'fruit and veg' was really not important for anyone to know, and they certainly knew and researched in great detail every aspect of the horticultural world they moved in, which was considered much to their credit.

The show would be introduced by a different member of the production team each evening. The introduction was simple enough - "Good evening, and welcome to another show of Don't Squeeze my Plums, presented by the Pratt Brothers." However, for some reason or another, this could never be said without it prompting hysterical laughter, which in turn gave considerable amusement to listeners, and in particular Lady Belling and Mrs Bircher, who would be doubled up, gasping for air - just two among how many others who had tuned in to this most popular of shows.

Later that evening Mrs Bircher spotted someone through the telescope that Lady Belling had set up for stargazing as the night sky drew in. On taking a second look, and a much closer inspection, she recognised the figure of .... could it be Gregory? .... in the back garden of Sessile and Linda's property ....

Would the plans materialise for a Fete Extravaganza arranged and guarded in the utmost secrecy by Major Shoreshot? Had Howard and Douglas Pratt delivered a show worth listening to? What exactly was Gregory doing at Sessile and Linda's property, having only spoken to Linda a few days before? And the ice cold drink made earlier by Lady Belling .... was it perhaps not quite as soft as we first thought?

One thing is for sure .... Only time will tell ....

Chapter Four

Little in Number

Dr Stillwell had recently returned from his holiday abroad - which had been instigated by Nancy after she had witnessed a young man enter the surgery with a most painful leg injury only to observe the Doctor put on his spectacles upside down merely to gaze up the poorly boy's nose, whilst at the same time listening to his own heartbeat with the stethoscope, and simultaneously taking a blood pressure reading from the boy's mother who had accompanied him to the surgery. It had therefore been unhesitatingly and extraordinarily clear to see that a holiday was desperately needed by the Doctor. This was apparent not only to Nancy, but also to the young patient he was trying to console . . . .

By now, however, some of the patients awaiting attention from the Doctor, and languishing not-so-patiently in the newly refurbished and more comfortable waiting room, felt a strange and urgent compulsion to perform a most absurd type of rain dance.

Nancy had taken it upon herself to reserve a flight on the Doctor's behalf. A change of scenery would do him good, she thought. It had been three years since Dr Stillwell had taken over the practice, only to discover that a great number of the interesting patients he had looked forward to caring for were either just about to die or, indeed, were dead already. All the same, he had worked tirelessly over those years to establish a new clientele from the diminished list left by the previous doctor, boozy old Dr Jameson. Nancy was always one to put aside trepidation at all times in favour of unrestrained encouragement and reassurance to those who needed it - even the most dispirited and disillusioned - despite which Dr Stillwell still found it most daunting to re-enter the surgery after his holiday.

"Did I see your father at the airfield today, Nancy?" asked Dr Stillwell.

"Probably. Was there a new twin prop in military colours readily available?"

"Yes."

"That would have been him then," Nancy replied.

"It's just that Nigel pointed out the plane to me as I disembarked from my flight. Have you ever met Nigel?" the Doctor enquired.

"Yes - in fact, only recently," she said . . . . with the hugest smile delivered through the most perfectly proportioned teeth of the brightest white imaginable. "I'll tell you all about it a little later," she said - a comment which planted an expression of complete bafflement on the face of the poor Doctor.

He had experienced the smoothest of landings executed by an extremely competent pilot who was more than capable of dealing with the strongest of the cross winds that had blown continually from the south for the last five days. On leaving the plane he had noticed his luggage being transported in a most peculiar manner, and had realised that it was Nigel who operated the tricycle used to load and unload passenger baggage. The tricycle sported a basket of much larger proportion than would normally be used, which trailed behind the tricycle, hitched to it by what could best be described as a makeshift hook and eye system which, nevertheless, worked more than adequately since Nigel had taken control of the grass airfield. Loading and unloading occurred twice daily, ferrying outgoing and incoming baggage to and from the waiting aircraft. However, as a result of Nigel's recent unfortunate attack, the fifty two second cycle ride to the aircraft from Departure Lounge Number One (out of a total of one!) had this time taken him over four minutes owing to his definitely diminished ability to cycle in a straight line, coupled with a unique and unruly pedalling technique, the extraordinary gyrations of which left in its wake an intricately carved crop circle pattern on the freshly cut landing strip. Nevertheless, without waiting to catch his breath from the outward adventure, he had started back without delay - complete with the additional weight imposed by passengers who had chosen to sit on top of the suitcases he had placed so carefully in the basket.

On opening the door for the Doctor, Nigel had walked across the Arrivals Suite with energetic enthusiasm to make a fresh pot of tea. However, once again his legs had given way completely and he had collapsed on the floor without ever reaching the tap, let alone making the tea. Dr Stillwell had then spent two or three seconds shaking Nigel, only to hear him repeat over and over again the one word, "Nancy . . . . Nancy . . .".

The following morning Gregory announced his presence at Sessile and Linda's house with the thunderous sound of a British hand-built driving machine - unrivalled, the very best, with full Prince of Wales specification. This man drove an Aston Martin Vantage Volante and, as the sun shone on the monstrous bonnet, its reflection bounced off straight into the open shower room window where Linda, finishing her morning ablutions and now in the throes of drying herself thoroughly where normally no light would enter, was suddenly brilliantly floodlit, courtesy of the angle at which the Aston was parked relative to the sunshine. Gregory - always a gentleman - turned a blind eye but was nonetheless completely aware that Linda had just started to apply moisturising lotion to her perfectly tanned and proportioned body .... which could not have been easy for Gregory, whose wife was currently fulfilling a lifelong ambition to command an expedition to one of the furthermost reaches of the earth - the North Pole!

As Gregory knocked on the solid oak door of this delightful property, he could barely contain his excitement because the green light had been given by the local authorities by way of their confirmation that any water flowing through private land was deemed to be in the ownership of that private landowner, provided that it emanated from a natural source. So, Gregory now realised that this was the answer to a problem that had robbed him of sleep for the last three nights - two of which he had spent in this garden, checking the apparatus he used to verify each time that the reading of the night before was correct. So .... this is why Mrs Bircher had spied him through Lady Belling's telescope .... which just goes to show that we cannot always trust our own eyes to make snap judgements!

This finely tuned piece of apparatus worked on a principle similar to a submarine sonar, producing a small shock wave that bounced back from its source, finally giving a basic graph reading to enable the user to pinpoint accurately the course followed by underground water. However, the equipment could not be used in direct sunlight, something to do with solar flares recurring at increasingly regular intervals - particularly throughout the last week although for obvious reasons not visible to the naked eye - which would have interfered with the sensitive and delicate electronics encased within the apparatus. Gregory was now able, with this information, to present a rational argument to the authorities, ultimately leading to a submission and, in due course, an agreement from them that the water could be used for any agricultural or horticultural purposes, provided that applications remained within the guidelines drawn up by the Governing Body. But the most astonishing fact - which remained constant throughout all four previous determination meetings attended by Gregory - was that the authorities in question were always little in number . . . .

Sessile and Linda had taken ownership of their lovely house in the October of the year before, following one of the wettest twelve months on record, although they did not take up residency until the following March, and were made very welcome at the earliest opportunity by PC Paul Ovary in the April, as mentioned earlier. Paul had been somewhat aware that water levels had reached worrying heights as rain continued to fall. Indeed, he had spoken to Sessile several times over the telephone, warning that the well was extraordinarily close to overflowing although, thankfully, the rains and the water level began to subside before this actually happened. The house itself had been owned previously by Dr Jameson, who had now chosen to move in with his sister who lived in that small and little known hamlet of Pigsmellwell. This move happened after his partner in the practice - Dr Stillwell - had made him a proposition on the basis that, if he were to take premature retirement, he would continue to run the surgery in a manner familiar to the clientele

.... It would be no exaggeration to say that Dr Stillwell, having paid an undisclosed sum of money for the practice, must have felt suicidal at times, and would doubtless have suffered far more were it not for his saving grace, the lovely Nancy.

Clive, in the meantime, made the decision to start an embroidery and tapestry class. The classes started after he closed the shop. Never one to wear a watch, he was governed by the sun and, once the village signpost lost its sun to the beckoning evening, the classes would commence. These took place in his store room on Tuesday and Friday nights - a seven week course that also included dressmaking and perfume application. The courses had grown in popularity - so much so that, in the first two weeks, he had to move to the small rear garden adjoining the shop, accessible only from the gate his grandfather had hung some eighty seven years before. This area was just about large enough to cater for the mammoth tapestry that Clive had started some weeks before for the Grand Reopening of The Pieced and Broke Arms. Its astonishing composition and design was left outside each day to create an aged appearance from the blisteringly hot sun. It was a truly marvellous piece of work, to which all his students wished to contribute. If Clive were given a needle and thread, his performance would be on a par with that of the finest of pianists, a startling and vibrant display of panache and fluidity for his students - who were totally and understandably in awe of this reserved and most respectful, gentle man - to pore and wonder over.

The Major had joined Gregory, Sessile and Linda in the back garden of their property, and was tightening the penultimate screw in the last panel of the self-driven motor to be used to collect and distribute the precious water so urgently needed for the hops. Gregory - a self-made millionaire - had made his fortune after leaving the university, where he had taught Miss Ploughman on occasions, to engage in a career change and enter the world of engineering. He had studied this subject in his youth, obtaining a Masters degree and specialising exclusively in magnetism, in the doing of which he had shaped an engine that ran on a magnetic pulse and required no fossil fuels. Technical and mathematical equations slept in the mind of this genius!

How did Linda Lillycrap have such an even all-over tan, and what exactly was Naturists' Monthly doing on the small round table in her entrance hall? Will the Major finish the last panel of the magnetically driven motor that works similarly to a water mill before Lady Belling returns home from her cottage? And just why in any case did she have that colossal telescope pointing in the direction of Well Bottled? Finally, how did the young boy make a full recovery so quickly from his leg injury as he skipped down Laid Out Lane?

Chapter Five

At Long Last

Miss Ploughman was now living in a possessed state of mind, having been promised by her supplier that the replacement door for The Pieced and Broke Arms' main fire escape would be with her well before the Unofficial Reopening date, which was set for the last Friday of this inconceivably oppressive month. Typically not one to become rattled - more harmonious than anything else - she was now ready to unleash a fury not unlike a nuclear explosion! A foolhardy person it would be to cross this woman in this condition at this moment in time. As luck would have it, however, before this eruption had a chance to occur, Tiberius walked into The Pieced and Broke Arms with the good news that not only had the rear beer garden been completed, but also his company was about to start the beginning of the end of the front drinking and dining areas.

Tiberius, although now retired from his aviation years, still had a hunger to work. His wife Isabella and their youngest daughter Tahlia had set up a gardening company nine months prior to his retirement to keep him occupied and, as a consequence, within fifteen weeks it had grown to such a size that its expansion fashioned a long chain of franchises and, in doing so, devoured any opposition that stood in its way. The Company was originally recommended to the Committee by Miss Ploughman via Nancy although she, being the firstborn of the family, was entirely devoted to her nursing and wished to have nothing to do with the Company at this current period of her life. The name for the now limited Company came out of the blue one evening - a suggestion put forward by Tahlia to use the first initial from each of their names .... Tiberius followed by Isabella and, finally, Tahlia - which left them with "Tits Gardening" and, of course, ended up with them all rolling around the floor in tears of laughter, nearly causing Isabella to have a stroke!

Shortly after Tiberius had walked into The Pieced and Broke Arms the telephone rang with even better news that the door, without a shadow of doubt, was ready and would be delivered first thing the following morning. Miss Ploughman now gave an enormous sigh of relief, and immediately her face lost the tension it had been wearing for a considerable time.

"At long last!" she shrieked .... and promptly poured herself a generous drink - and well deserved it was for she had been at the end of her tether since the excuses given to her from the manufacturers were less than justifiable. Miss Ploughman's intuition told her that the delay may have been intentional, having dealt with them in the past, which probably contributed to the reason why she would not any longer continue to tolerate their incompetence and unprofessional conduct.

Mrs Bircher and Lady Belling had taken an alternative route home from their normal path after their five-day break at Pigsmellwell, to have their hair attended to. Mrs Bircher had introduced Lady Belling several weeks before to her hair stylist - a flamboyant and dramatic salon owner - and had eventually persuaded her to make an advance booking, having herself been one of the salon's most devoted and loyal clients.

Richard and Francesca - a husband and wife team - had attended to Mrs Bircher's needs for the last eighteen years or so, always with complete satisfaction. The business itself had been built on a reputation for creative and imaginative work, but still had the original sign - Dick and Fanny's Hair Emporium - which really did not do them justice. Richard, an ex-basketball player at a height of six foot seven inches, towered above his wife Francesca, but was nonetheless continually controlled by her venomous tongue insisting, for one thing, that all members of staff were to wear uniforms reminiscent of a science fiction show broadcast on the television many years before. Moreover, if the uniform provided by the salon for the male and female gender was not maintained continually in absolutely pristine condition, there would be a heavy price to pay.

Lady Belling and Mrs Bircher had put their inquisitive heads around the main door of The Pieced and Broke Arms to observe how things were coming along for the Unofficial Reopening, looking equally very well-rested and refreshed. Mrs Bircher, being something of a sleeping partner within the Committee, was nevertheless one of the largest shareholders of this project and sat on the Board of Directors. She preferred to take more of a back seat with the goings-on that were taking place but, if ever she was needed, a tour de force of conviction she would be - a more reliable and dependable person would be impossible to find.

Isabella, accompanied by Tahlia, had walked the perimeter of the hopfields that afternoon and, in doing so, had become more acquainted with the Major as he was in the midst of laying the final hose that would dripfeed water to the hops through an ingeniously designed system drawn up by Gregory. This would deliver an abundance of water for the hops when needed, from the well that lay at the end of Sessile and Linda's garden. The well water would be brought to the surface by the principal magnetic motor which would then run in a sequence, passing through an array of pipes and hoses to the sub self-driven magnetic motors, and be pumped from there to its final destination, where it would drip from the pipes at varying intervals up and down the rows throughout the day to replenish the hops . . . . All that now remained was to put the wheels in motion and turn it on while the well remained over half full.

PC Paul Ovary was on his way to the nearest Police Station some distance away from Well Bottled, where his Bravery Award was waiting to be presented to him by Sergeant

Simmons for "outstanding action above and beyond the call of duty" some time before he had moved to the village. Paul had single-handedly taken on three men - the first being wheelchair-bound, the second who had double vision, and the third and most dangerous with impaired hearing (in fact he was completely deaf) - but this did not deter Paul after being tipped off that these three were somewhere in the vicinity and had been the main suspects for some time for a number of criminal offences. The Police had tried to track down these tyrants for the last two years for one of the most despicable of crimes, but Paul had managed to catch them red-handed in the appalling act of Knock Down Ginger, having chased all three suspects along narrow alleyways, through neglected allotments and freshly tarmac'd driveways. Nevertheless, he successfully apprehended all three .... Trevor the Taper, Wilfred the Whistler and, most notorious of them all, Stevie the Sparkler, who had a tendency to set light to his own fingers which made it difficult for the Police to get any decent prints. Stevie, in particular, had laid low for the first six months of that year. On returning to his escapades he had got wedged between a rabbit hutch and an aviary while trying to make a quick getaway after, yet again, performing this most horrid of dirty deeds - only to be restrained by none other than PC Paul Ovary. Trevor and Wilfred, on the other hand, gave themselves up without any sort of resistance.

As if Miss Ploughman had not had enough good news for one day, she had an unexpected surprise delivery of embroidered uniforms - an order she had placed with Clive some weeks ago that he managed to despatch ten days earlier than expected with help from his Friday class. These included a motif on the shirt sleeves, trouser pockets and waistcoat lapels, while on the back would be a listing of the beers available, including a brand new one that had just reached fermentation and was in the process of being bottled. This was the strongest beer ever produced by The Pieced and Broke Arms *issers, a potent concoction best sipped in small doses rather than consumed in its entirety, with a name giving an idea of its strength - Nelson's Right Arm. This name came into being after five Committee members were selected for a comprehensive but largely experimental tasting session of the new beer at the distillery, only to discover on reaching the halfway mark of their third pint that each and every one of them felt as if he had lost a limb - a feeling that inexplicably led to an eventual numbness of the upper torso. This beer really was rocket fuel!

PC Paul Ovary was the first to arrive at Police Headquarters and, as a result, was placed at the front of the line-up which included twelve other policemen and women who were about to receive the Honorary Handcuff Medal, as well as a special surprise gift from Sergeant Simmons. In Paul's case this was a book he had often spoken about but, up until now, had never come across -One Hundred and One Shiniest Policemen's' Helmets - this came as a most pleasant surprise for Paul.

Meanwhile, Clive's twice-weekly classes had grown so much in popularity that now he was finding it more difficult than ever to keep up with demand, so he placed an advertisement in Well Bottled Weekly for an assistant to help with the Tuesday night embroidery class that he was struggling to cope with, with the additional pressure it entailed. The free newspaper was posted on Monday evenings by the young boy with the not-so-severe leg injury, shortly before the ever-increasingly listened-to radio show, Don't Squeeze my Plums.

Nancy's family was now in the fourth day of their two-week stay - which at times seemed to be more of a busman's holiday than fourteen days of rest. Tahlia was becoming a little concerned that her parents - particularly her father - would work continuously throughout this fortnight, so she was utterly delighted to hear him announce, as he walked through Nancy's front door grasping a copy of Well Bottled Weekly, that Tits Gardening had just completed the grounds of The Pieced and Broke Arms, and all that remained now was to ensure that Committee members were happy with the works the company had carried out. He sat down on one of the kitchen chairs, where the table had been laid earlier by Tahlia, while Isabella was preparing the evening meal ready for the family - although they would have to wait a little longer since Nancy had been on call for most of the day and had yet to return home, having encountered one of her patients refusing to come down from the large elm tree at the end of Laid Out Lane to take his medication.

As Tiberius flicked through the pages of the paper, Dahlia came through the door that led from the living room into the kitchen and sat on the dining chair opposite her father.

"I overheard what you said as you came in, and I'm really pleased you've finished the grounds of the Pub. Maybe now you can have ten days of complete relaxation, Daddy", she said.

"Yes, it's all finished", he said as he kicked off his shoes and sat back in a more slumbering fashion, giving a most reassuring wink at his beautiful daughter.

"Oh, by the way, do you still work on any of those tapestries now like you used to?" he asked.

"No, not for an awfully long time. What made you say that Daddy?" she replied inquisitively.

"Well, in this publication of Well Bottled Weekly there's an advertisement for help desperately needed for an embroidery class this coming Tuesday, and I instinctively thought of you, knowing how fidgety you become on holiday - and, looking at you, I think you may already have had enough sun!"

"Can I have a look?" she asked. "Okay, I'll give it some thought."

Tahlia, an absolute sun worshipper, was already sunkissed on her arrival in Well Bottled but, having applied Nancy's formula sun protection lotion for the last two days, was currently the darkest shade of mahogany I had ever seen! .... But, my goodness, she looked absolutely breathtaking.

Will the new fire escape door arrive for Miss Ploughman, as promised and on time? Can we expect the turning-on of the irrigation system to go without a hitch? Why was Sergeant Simmons so red in the face as he presented Paul Ovary with his book? And just what did happen to the plans made by Major Shoreshot for a Fete Extravaganza?

Chapter Six

An Opportunity

The next morning Major Shoreshot was up an hour earlier than usual, awaiting delivery of the new fire escape door, only to find himself pleasantly surprised to hear the sound of the lorry approaching in the distance as it wove its way along Laid Out Lane on this scorchingly hot Saturday morning. The Major was positioned ready, standing in the ideal location to guide the vehicle through the newly constructed archway that led to the entrance of the car parking area of The Pieced and Broke Arms. This was going to be an awkward manoeuvre to accomplish on the driver's behalf. Miss Ploughman, however, had been assured that the company would provide the very best driver available for this delivery.

"Where is Paul?" shouted Miss Ploughman to the Major from across the other side of the car park, having arranged with him to be in attendance.

"No idea", said the Major. "Was he meant to be here?"

"Yes, of course he was!"

As these words left her mouth, the delivery lorry made its final approach along the narrowest part of Laid Out Lane, and only then did they eyewitness Paul hurtling past at the rate of knots on his new Police pushbike, screaming that the brake cable had snapped. The bike was the very latest the Police had to offer to all its village PCs . . . . and was supposed to encourage the public to cycle to and from their destinations as opposed to using their cars in this type of rural environment. Fortunately for Paul, the pushbike came supplied with a reinforced, comfort-fit chequered-flag, Police regulation crash helmet that also incorporated integral flashing lights, as well as many other additional features. . . . including a high-powered multi-functional siren that sat comfortably on the handlebars; indicators; a high definition satellite navigation system; a comprehensive first aid kit; flares; pressurised pump; and . . . . the most magnificent feature of all . . . . the No-Numb-Bum saddle. This bike really was Paul's pride and joy.

Shortly after five o'clock on that Saturday afternoon Linda returned home from Dick and Fanny's Hair Emporium, having had her eighth botox injection and now looking as if she were standing in a wind tunnel on a permanent basis. Linda really did look most peculiar but, just inside that passing hour, a vast amount of swelling had now begun to subside and a noticeable improvement in her speech did not go unnoticed. Her ears and eyes also became more visible and the nasal congestion, thankfully, became less evident. There was, however, one minute problem in that, every time Linda smiled, the corners of her mouth reached her forehead. Sessile, in the meantime, was in the middle of putting the finishing touches to his evening attire and, on vacating the dressing room, found himself confronted by his wife, which gave him the fright of his life! "Surely that liquor I consumed earlier wasn't that strong?' he thought to himself.

"Have you had one of those wretched botox injections again, darling?" he asked.

"Yes, what do you think?"

"Well, it looks a little unusual at the moment, but I'm sure when the swelling completely subsides your face will look as adorable as always."

"Well, do you think I should put the ice bag on it? .... because Gregory is due to arrive at seven thirty and he might think I've fallen into a beehive!" said Linda in a progressively more worried way.

"Gregory would not be concerned in the least with your appearance tonight - he already has enough on his mind to think about; and even if he did notice I'm sure he wouldn't mention it, so try not to concern yourself unnecessarily."

That Saturday evening was the date set for the turning-on of the irrigation system, and two very special guests had been approached by the Committee to attend officially and take part in the switching-on ceremony. A correspondence of acceptance had been received the previous day by the Committee, which said in short that the Pratt Brothers would be honoured to attend.

This produced a profound effect on some of the more mature members of the Committee, many of whom had burst into a most uncharacteristic state of frenzy. Arthur in particular, now ninety two years young, resembled a rabid dog - he who had been Head Gardener for Lady Belling on the estate after servicing the needs of her father, Earl Guthrie Belling, many years before until that gentleman's untimely death linked with occupied allied territories. Thank goodness, the only thing ever to have been acknowledged on the subject over the years was the astonishing story of an extrovert French maid about an oversized feather duster, some very out-of-the-ordinary cleaning apparatus, a fluffy bunny-rabbit ear collection, still boxed and in full working order, and lastly - though least mentioned of all - the largest chocolate muffins ever seen in modern history.

Sessile had spent the best part of the day preparing his home-made sauce as an accompaniment to the Beggars' Banquet in which he had specialised at catering college as a young man. Although rarely found in the kitchen these days, he genuinely enjoyed the sense of fulfilment in accomplishing this hugely excessive and most sumptuous presentation; however, this fact had never once been recognised or acknowledged by his tutors throughout the years he spent at college, which had resulted in a feeling of injustice that rarely left Sessile, together with the continually recurring dream of putting the main tutor in the deep fat fryer and shutting the lid until the onion rings were a deep shade of crispy brown!

It was now seven thirty, as the door knocker struck Sessile and Linda's solid oak front door.

"That will be Gregory. Sessile, can you get the front door?"

"Yes . . . . okay . . . . will do."

"Good evening Sessile", said Gregory, swiftly followed by, "I say, something smells rather good. Who's been in the kitchen?"

"That would have to be me," replied Sessile in a very sheepish manner.

Gregory, however, had brought with him some terrific news, unbeknown to Sessile and Linda. Having spoken to the Board of Directors, Gregory had requested that Sessile and Linda be incorporated into the Committee. The vote went unanimously and unhesitatingly in their favour following consideration of Gregory's most inspiring and influential pitch and, as a result, Sessile and Linda would be receiving an equal share owing to the immense help they had both become over the last few weeks, and the considerate, unassuming attitude and over-riding mutual commitment both had displayed from beginning to end in facilitating this desperate need.

The grandmother clock struck eight as Isabella looked up the newly polished staircase in Nancy's cottage to discover the whereabouts of Tahlia.

"Come on darling," she called with a sense of urgency. "We'll be late if you don't hurry!"

"I'm just applying my perfume. Give me one moment and I'll be with you," answered Tahlia in a most moderate way from her now more-than-ever succulent-looking lips.

"What time do you think Nancy will be there, Mummy?" asked Tahlia as she glided her way down the staircase in a dress fit only for the angelic . . . . and this dress really did not waste any material. Tahlia was an absolute vision of beauty supreme, flanked either side by the most delicate scent that left one chasing the presence of a vapour trail that seemed to follow her gorgeousness. It would be an extremely lucky man to take this divine creature's hand.

The Major and Miss Ploughman were just about to make the short journey from The Pieced and Broke Arms to Sessile and Linda's house, only to find themselves stopped in their tracks by Lady Belling and Mrs Bircher as they were locking the newly installed fire escape door, that had been fitted with the utmost care earlier in the day by the most obliging delivery driver that the two of them had ever met - one Maxi-Million-Axiom, who had a perpetual desire to drive his chariot in costume. The number plate . . . . 121 ROME . . . . should have given some sort of indication of what was to come, but nothing could nor would have prepared them for what would happen next. As Maxi-Million-Axiom exited the massive lorry cab, his sword dangled liberally in the gusting summer breeze and, unfortunately for Maxi, at the same time his toga lifted from just above his knees to well above his head as an unexpected updraft of air swirled up his inner thigh, exposing the twelve-inch razor-sharp sheath knife held securely in place by the leather garter .... which left very little to the imagination .... Nevertheless, there was no doubt that this trucker had no need of a German Shepherd for protection!

Many Committee members had made their way to Sessile and Linda's house as dusk began to roll in under an astonishing midnight blue colour sky with occasional dancing shimmers of green light over the far horizon .... once again, this apparently had something to do with the solar flares that were about to reach their peak by midnight. As Lady Belling was strolling across the lower end of Laid Out Lane with Miss Ploughman, Major Shoreshot and Mrs Bircher, she suddenly remembered that her telescope had been left in the cottage at Pigsmellwell, and was absolutely furious with herself.

"Oh, bloody hell!" she said.

"What on earth is wrong, old girl?" asked the Major.

"I've only gone and left the telescope at the cottage", she said, with a ferocity most unlike her.

Lady Belling had been awaiting this magical event for a number of months, and the conditions could not have been better to see the night sky lit so brightly by the flares - an opportunity that happened only once in a lifetime. The telescope itself had been a gift for Lady Belling's sixty fifth birthday from the Major, knowing how fascinated she had been from a young child with astrology and astronomy. Little did she know that the Major, if truth were told, had already positioned her telescope in a fantastic place at the end of Sessile and Linda's porch which overlooked the hopfields and beyond, from there, to the expanse of open sky.

As all four of them came within earshot of Sessile and Linda's house, they began to hear the distinctive sound of camaraderie as the gathering was building momentum, mainly because Douglas and Howard Pratt had turned up in their nephew's van having had a puncture - nothing strange in that, except that the nephew was in fact a fishmonger, and the signwriting on the van read Shellfish, Pratt & Son . . . . and this justifiably sent everyone into a state of unreserved hysteria!

The Major meanwhile, a crack shot with an arrow, had made arrangements with Linda - and Linda alone - that he would announce his arrival by shooting her from three hundred and sixty four paces! Linda, of course, was prepared and was dressed in a protective vest hidden under her clothing, which had been supplied by the Major two days earlier with no-one being any the wiser. The vest had been part of his regiment's special forces kit, and the Major had been longing for an occasion to dust down this highly regarded piece of life-saving equipment and put it to use for one last time. The idea was for Linda to walk from the porch down five of the nine steps to the garden as he shot her straight in the chest! This, in turn, would trigger the automated remote sensor in the vest, causing a chain reaction to commence, starting with the water being pumped from the well to all the waiting hoses and pipes that would then begin to replenish the hops, and ending with forty or so firework rockets going up in succession at the far end of the hopfield.

Quite understandably, neither Paul nor Nigel would be attending .... Paul because of the cycling incident that morning, although his fiancée had been informed that the twenty three per cent bruising sustained throughout his body would heal, given time. Rosina, however, had decided to fly straight to the nearby airfield that afternoon by Police helicopter. A policewoman herself, she went by the name of Rosina the Screamer . . . . but the less said about that the better! Nigel, on the other hand, was being looked after by none other than Nancy after his last attack of Knocking Knee Syndrome at the airfield.

Does Clive eat all of the cous-cous and aduki bean pie with the one-inch houmous topping? Will the self-exploding arrow tip, filled with tomato ketchup, work as it hits Linda in the chest? How will Lady Belling react on knowing her telescope is already in the best position to see the solar flares? And at just what time can we expect Nancy's entrance to take place at the Beggars' Banquet?

Chapter Seven

Finally

The count-down was nearly over for next Friday's Unofficial Reopening of The Pieced and Broke Arms on the Monday morning following the Beggars' Banquet - now having become more a number of days than of weeks. Yet a soothing atmosphere seemed to encircle the village that morning as the sun rose and began to shine directly through the Surgery's large glass window that stood at the east end of the green. Here, at this stifling break of day, as beads of perspiration began to weep from his brow, Dr Stillwell now looked more hawk-eyed than ever before having spent the best part of the last two nights coming to terms with the knowledge that his balls had finally dropped. Time and time again he had come so close but, on that Saturday night of all nights, they fell with the numbers he had always used from the very first time he developed an appetite for playing the lottery and, on checking his ticket for the thirteenth time, he discovered that he had scooped himself a cool £9,125,743.08 .... Yes .. It was true! .... Nine million, one hundred and twenty five thousand, seven hundred and forty three pounds, and eight pence!

Nigel's situation had also improved, although he still drifted in and out of consciousness, was not the least bit coherent and made little sense. But he had remained adamant in wearing his soft kid leather flying helmet, goggles and lucky flying scarf throughout another of his distressing spells although this time, having begun to regain some sort of movement to his legs, the troublesome knees that had plagued him so continually had remained completely and utterly stationary throughout the attack.

The Doctor, although in frequent contact with Nancy during this trying time, had found it too challenging to draw himself away from his winning ticket and, as a result, Nancy had not been able to attend the Beggars' Banquet on the Saturday night. Not once, however, had the thought entered her mind to leave Nigel's side, for she had felt bound by a sense of duty and it would have taken wild horses to tear this nurse away from the needs of this desperate man.

It had been with the utmost of good intentions that Nancy had taken the time not only to take care of Nigel's health, but also to ensure that his clothing was pressed and ready to wear upon his recovery. Nonetheless, on hanging his jacket in the wardrobe, she had inadvertently stumbled across a partially opened envelope which had fallen to the floor and, on returning it whence it had fallen, to the inner pocket of the right hand side of Nigel's jacket, she had noticed a folded piece of paper and, assuming that this must have come adrift from its accompanying envelope, had felt it imperative that she return it to its rightful place - with the purest of intentions and without plan or purpose of what she would do later that evening. Somehow, however, she had felt bothered by the oxidized and stained envelope for much of the time through the long hours of darkness that had encompassed her while she cared for Nigel … but Nancy felt very strongly about this sort of thing and she was not one to break her own rules on privacy. However, in this instance, she had found herself battling against her own deep convictions, even wondering whether possibly, enclosed within that letter, there might be some sort of explanation to Nigel's continually troubled mind and the problems that seemed to have played an increasingly commanding role in the recent years of his life.

Eventually, after fighting a losing battle with her own judgement, Nancy had found favour with the inquisitive side of her nature and, in that passing moment, had caught sight of her reflection in the full-length mirror on the wardrobe door and had seen herself reading the intimate handwritten poetry, sealed with a kiss, that Nigel had written some eleven years before after being jilted at the altar by the woman he had always longed to marry . . . . Samantha!

At this stage on that Monday morning, Clive was waiting very patiently outside the surgery - in the most agitated manner and in desperate need of some attention and relief from his most uncomfortable symptoms. There was only one person to whom he could refer this embarrassing problem and who could provide a most needed solution, and that was Dr Stillwell. Clive had spent over twenty five hours on the toilet, having himself eaten more than three quarters of the cous-cous and aduki bean pie with the one-inch houmous topping on the Saturday evening, and then washed it down by way of three pints of Puddle of Piddle and half a pint of The Squirrel's Nuts and then, unwisely, finishing off with two more half pints of the strongest brew .... Nelson's Right Arm! It had been at this exact moment, on taking his last mouthful of this liquid nitro, that Jahlia had followed her parents through the double-glazed French doors leading from the sitting room at the back of Sessile and Linda's house to the rear garden patio area where the merrymaking was well and truly under way. In that exact split second of time - on seeing this diva - Clive's jaw had fallen to the floor.

"Oh, do close your mouth, Clive.... And while you're at it, try and put your eyes back in your head and your tongue away", Sessile had said as he walked past the Beggars' Banquet table while Clive took hold of the candelabra in an effort to steady himself.

Instantaneously, Clive had made the monumental decision to introduce himself to a woman whose company he had only ever dreamt of sharing but, in standing up from the table, the realisation had just hit him.... What with the amount of pie and beer he had consumed it was within less than four seconds that his stomach had begun to make a sound reminiscent of some sort of Edwardian plumbing: moreover, as he had stood at the side of the table, it had swollen to such a size that he looked as if he were expecting ... twins! On excusing himself from the table, and leaving the house through the side door in extremely hurried fashion, Clive had expelled sufficient methane to power two small farms, shortly followed by a plentiful and most satisfactory delivery of manure, enough to cover over four good-sized parcels of land. He was by then in the most frightful state, and just barely able to walk!

Clive arrived at the Surgery from his shop in the early hours of this momentous Monday morning in mind-boggling time - and in a style not far removed from that of someone with a severe case of St Vitus' Dance, combined with that of a long-distance speed walker. He could scarcely make out the figure of Dr Stillwell, diffused through the frosted window to the left of the entrance door of the Surgery, who seemed to be holding a piece of paper in exact alignment to the streaming sunlight that poured through the window, which might have given the impression that he was kissing his winning ticket in the most exaggerated manner! In fact, he was in the throes of cleaning an X-ray he had been studying the day before, and was in the midst of blowing the small particles of excess dust from the now ticket-sized negative of the cross-section which was enlarged to about four times its original size. It was this particular subdivision of the X-ray that held an element of fascination for Dr Stillwell.

During all of this, Gregory had been in contact with as many media companies as he could bring to mind (and, believe me, that was quite a few!) that he felt might have an interest in the coming together of the good people of Well Bottled and the birth of a new era from a very chequered past. Now was the time for Gregory to unleash his leviathan expertise in this field, an area that he knew like the back of his hand. (In other words, both of his sisters had very high-powered jobs in the media world, one being a freelance journalist for a number of recognised tabloids, while the other was head of a very well-known television station . . . . in fact, having achieved executive status, she virtually ran the whole European network more or less by herself, and the world really was her oyster!)

Rosina had been telephoned direct on the personal outbound line from Regional Headquarters by Chief Superintendent Lord Collier, enquiring as to her whereabouts as there was a crisis at the Special Branch School and he had been trying to get hold of her to help try and ease the situation there, since Sergeant Simmons had achieved less than a little control over the outbreak of compulsive shoe polishing! Paul, however, had asked her already if she would be willing to take over traffic control for the forthcoming Unofficial Reopening of The Pieced and Broke Arms the following Friday, as he was still suffering in silence from his internal bruising following the cycling incident.

Richard and Francesca had arranged for two coach loads of their vast clientele to be arriving at The Pieced and Broke Arms between five thirty and six o'clock for the first sitting of a four course dinner set up by Miss Ploughman. The second sitting would commence at eight o'clock on the dot, which meant there would be very little room for error while running such a tight schedule…. as Miss Ploughman explained in full detail to the new members of staff after they had all tried on their new uniforms - and really very smart and professional they looked, not only in appearance but also in conduct. Miss Ploughman was most pleased.

By the time night fell on that day, Nancy felt she had accomplished as much as she could for Nigel, having left him in the capable hands of Dr

Stillwell. She was now absolutely exhausted and drained, even finding it incredibly difficult to walk home, let alone anything else! However, as she hung her traditional nursing headwear on the allocated hook behind the back door that was always used for this item, she found a note on the kitchen table giving detailed instructions that, if she were to turn around and face the fridge, a surprise was in store for her .... which she promptly did ... to find yet another note that read, "Open me immediately!" On opening the fridge door as instructed she found, thanks to her sister Tahlia, an excellently prepared and presented home-made seafood platter, accompanied by a chilled bottle of white wine with an outstanding lineage .... ready and waiting for her consumption.

Tahlia, however, was nowhere to be seen as she had replied to the advertisement that requested a helping hand for that Tuesday

night's embroidery and tapestry class. Having
rung the number several times, she had decided
to walk down to The Pieced and Broke Arms
straight from Nancy's cottage to try to find an
answer with regard to the advertisement that
had been placed in Well Bottled Weekly the
week before. As she walked through the open
door of the Pub, she was greeted by Melvin,
a mynah bird that Rosina had presented to
Miss Ploughman as a kindly gesture! The
bird's keeper had been none other than Paul but
now, with cutbacks in the Police Force, he could
not dedicate the amount of time to Melvin that
he deserved .... although in the beginning they
had both enjoyed many re-runs of 'Cops and
Robbers' shows from the 1970s. Unfortunately
there was a down side to this arrangement in that
Melvin had picked up a most distasteful use
of the English language, as well as the ability
to mimic most things, including a number of

undesirable bodily functions! Melvin, despite his apparent self-assurance, had missed Paul's company and had taken to pulling out his feathers through loneliness, and Paul realised in time that there was a strong possibility that Melvin could quite possibly pluck himself to death! .... and, even just thinking about it, he knew he would never be able to live with himself if this were to happen.

Why did Clive eat so much aduki bean pie? What exactly was in that X-ray that the doctor found so intriguing? Was it because Lord Collier was Rosina's godfather that he allowed her to take an additional two weeks of leave? Just why was it that Linda still looked as if she were sucking on a lemon, although the majority of swelling had now subsided? Will Melvin learn to behave in The Pieced and Broke Arms? And what will Dr Stillwell do with his new-found millions?

Chapter Eight

The Extravaganza

Mrs Bircher had travelled the long journey to the distant city of Higher Spire, to have a business lunch with a close old friend of the late Dr Reverend Bircher, Herbert Harris, who - it must be said - was now on a slippery slope as he rapidly approached retirement age, having spent his working life dealing with some of the most complicated mathematical equations. Herbert had built up an accomplished, respected - even revered - accountancy company over the many years of his career in this part of the British Isles - a practice that went by the encouraging name of Tax Evasions Limited UK.... which the Inland Revenue found none too joyous!

Lady Belling was also in the city of Higher Spire for the Grand Final of the forthcoming Campanology Championship that was to be judged by none other than Bishop Godfrey Goodie who, in the main, was a most pleasurable Bishop to have around. The event itself, more often than not, was taken very seriously, although there was always an underlying air of fun involved, particularly on this occasion when the Bishop threw down the gauntlet and took up the challenge of the guide rope swinging discipline in the hope of becoming the new holder of the.... Big Bells Cup. Unfortunately for Lady Belling, whose team had held the trophy for a number of years, it might not be quite such a foregone conclusion this year as to who would win the prized solid silver set of dumb-bells mounted on the twenty two carat gold plinth, owing to the fact that her two strongest and most important team members, Edwina and Harriet Armstrong, had inadvertently managed earlier in the day, whilst preparing for the competition, to entwine themselves in three of the bell leader ropes - so much so that they had to be taken away in a white van by four men in white coats to be . . . . unravelled!

Major Shoreshot had eventually managed to get in contact with Gregory - after spending most of the day trying and so putting a strenuous drain on the antiquated battery pack that powered the now obsolete, shoulder strap-held gargantuan mobile phone - with the stupendous news that the irrigation system was working better than they could ever have wished. The flip side of this good news was that the distillery producing the new range of beers had never been designed for this volume of production, and the overload was now causing a number of motors to burn out. These motors ran the belts which were now laden with a massive quantity of bottles and finding it difficult to cope with the additional weight and speed needed to keep up with demand, and this in turn had resulted in a slackening effect which became more and more problematical with each new outer it carried. The Major made a suggestion to Gregory that, if the Committee were in full agreement, two options might be considered. The first option, and dominant in the Major's mind, was to raze the existing building to the ground and utilise this expanse of land for a now desperately needed storage area, while at the same time transforming the waste land that remained either side and building a much more generously proportioned and productive distillery. The only other option would be to continue on the existing site just within the fringes of the village. If agreement could be reached by the Committee for the new triple-sized construction, it would remain completely screened by the original, now fully grown and established trees that enclosed the boundary of the site, thus keeping within the guidelines of the local council and the height restrictions that were still in place for this type of commercial construction.

"Oh, what to do, Mummy," were the first words spoken by Nancy as she awoke from her sixteen hours of slumber after the most upsetting couple of nights spent taking care of Nigel .... as her mother Isabella entered the third and smallest bedroom with a tray of piping hot, freshly made tea accompanied by a rack of lightly toasted wholemeal bread.

"What on earth is on your mind, my darling?" asked Isabella but, before she had a chance to answer, Tahlia walked in to see how her sister was feeling and to enquire if she had enjoyed the seafood platter that she had taken the time to prepare for her the night before.

Mrs Bircher had just caught up with Lady Belling after a fantastic lunch, courtesy of Herbert, who had given a projection for the year end profit and loss accounts for the first twelve months of trading of The Pieced and Broke Arms *issers, and whose in-depth forecast looked most encouraging for all concerned. In fact, Herbert was most impressed that all Committee members had taken the time to maintain such a detailed and itemised itinerary of the goings-on of the venture - even those who held the smallest number of shares, purchased on impulse at such a late stage, who nevertheless - and rightly - were regarded with the same importance as any other Committee member. Herbert was clearly very impressed.

"Did you get around to helping out at that embroidery and tapestry class, Sweetie?" asked Tiberius of his daughter Tahlia, who was now browner than brown, as they lay sunbathing on the shredded sunbaked grass of Nancy's back lawn at the halfway mark of that week.

"No, Daddy, though I did phone the number several times and no-one ever answered, so I decided to walk down to The Pieced and Broke Arms in the afternoon. I spoke with Miss Ploughman and she told me the person I needed to see was most unwell - somebody by the name of Clive. Do you know who he is, Daddy?"

"No, I don't think so, yet his name does seem to ring a bell. I may have met him, but I can't seem to put a face to the name."

"She also said he had been at the Beggars' Banquet - which is a shame because, had I known, it would have given me the opportunity to introduce myself to him. By the way, Daddy, I saw hardly anything of Nancy yesterday - actually, come to think of it, I only caught a glimpse of her this morning. Is she okay?"

"Yes, Nancy is absolutely fine. She's gone to see how Nigel is."

"Is that the Nigel you know from the airfield?"

"Yes, the same one, and according to your mother she seems to have become quite smitten with him.... Which is most unusual for Nancy, don't you think?"

"Actually, you're right there, come to think of it .... I can't recall Nancy ever allowing a patient to have an effect on her like this, especially one under her direct supervision," replied Dahlia with an air of mild bamboozlement.

As this conversation began to draw to a close, both Dahlia and Tiberius heard an

unbelievable sound coming from the direction
of the public footpath than ran at the back end
of Nancy's cottage and, as they stood up to see
what exactly all the commotion was about, they
were greeted by the shocking sight of Lady
Belling and Mrs Bircher, with a gigantic
bottle of well-known gin, drowning their sorrows
after losing the Big Bells Cup at the City of
Higher Spire Campanology Championship,
for this was the first time ever that they had not
held the trophy. However, the irony of this was
that they were also in the midst of celebrating
the good news of the huge profit made from the
first year's trading of The Pieced and Broke
Arms *'issers, and Lady Belling had tied
her stockings together to make a skipping rope,
while Mrs Bircher had removed her brassiere
and turned it into some sort of elasticated
slingshot. On closer inspection, Tiberius and
Tahlia could not help but notice that the ladies

appeared to be totally and utterly inebriated, as Mrs Bircher began flicking her slingshot bra at Lady Belling's buttocks. It was now unquestionably obvious that they were both completely intoxicated.

The penultimate day was now here, and Miss Ploughman was delighted with the mammoth tapestry that Clive had presented to her in private late the night before after making a full recovery from his bad turn after the Beggars Banquet. The now wall-mounted, eight by five foot masterpiece hung in pride of place - well above the open fire but below the vaulted ceiling - and looked absolutely stunning, with just the right amount of side and back lighting giving the illusion that the whole thing was about to come alive. The tapestry depicted the scene of a meeting between the Committee members, who sat around a stone, mediaeval-type round table, and behind the interactions taking place between these figures the background wall bore the title, carved in wood, of this wonderful creation - a title decided upon by Clive after weeks of long, hard thought. The chosen name was A Summer Talent.

Rosina had been asked to take over the authoritative role for the following morning after Paul had confirmed that he would not be well enough, despite everything, to take a leading part in the policing for the unofficial reopening of The Pieced and Broke Arms - but he would try his darnedest to be there despite still looking like a constipated duck when he walked! Major Shoreshot was none too happy that morning, having discovered his wife Lady Belling sprawled in the bath following the escapades she had got up to with Mrs Bircher the day before . . . . Lady Belling no doubt must have found it highly amusing at the time to leave an expensive bar of soap on the bathroom radiator - just long enough for it to melt into a very rude shape - and then to have stuck the obscene structure on her forehead. On the other hand, Mrs Bircher apparently must have thought it would be most comical to make a swing hammock from a number of her net curtains, and she could clearly be seen by all the villagers as she had not only used the ones that hid her living room from the outside world, but indeed had set the hammock up in that very same room - which was now open for all to see - with the gin bottle swinging variously and precariously alongside her!

With the help of twelve Committee members the Major managed to get virtually all of the bunting up in readiness for the Extravaganza that was to coincide with the Official Reopening of The Pieced and Broke Arms on the Saturday. He was hoping that this would be the best fete in the county, and was running around like a headless chicken in anticipation of what was to come. Normally a sedate and dignified type of chap, at one stage he felt his brains were literally going to explode with excitement! However, Rosina had been a great help to him throughout this day, marking out the spacers for the Eager Beaver Trail and the human-size catapult at the end of the imaginative, maze-like route - the idea was for the winner, ie the first to reach the end of the trail, to be catapulted back to the beginning to land safely into the large net set up by the entrance to the Trail. From there, if all went to plan, the ricochet effect should launch the winner onto a waiting trampoline to be presented with the Eager Beaver - a set of enormous front beaver teeth. Just one little thing remained for the winner to achieve before the award ceremony could take place, which was to lasso the teeth which would be hanging from the highest branch of the large elm tree at the bottom end of Laid Out Lane.

Why did Melvin keep saying to Miss Ploughman each morning, "Stop your grinning and drop your linen", after she gave him such a warm welcome - perhaps something to do with the unpolitically correct 1970s re-runs he had watched with PC Paul Ovary? What words had Nigel used in his poem to make Nancy fall to her knees on the night she disgraced herself by reading his most lovingly cared-for and treasured possession? Will Tahlia ever get the chance to meet Clive? And does the safety equipment set up by Major Shoreshot for the Fete Extravaganza work properly?

Chapter Nine

Ultimately

The Unofficial Reopening date was ultimately here, and Gregory was the first to appear at The Pieced and Broke Arms, having been lucky enough to enjoy a satellite-linked conversation with his wife and now knowing that she had achieved her lifelong ambition to reach the North Pole, aided by an incredibly supportive team who had accompanied her from beginning to end and encountered with her some of the most treacherous and dangerous environments known to Man! Gregory was absolutely euphoric by now, only then to hear her announce in addition that, after five days of rest in their bolthole constructed of ice and snow, they would begin the hazardous trek home! As ecstatic as he was on hearing this, Gregory continued to remain fully focussed on the job in hand and the forthcoming day's events, to assist his sisters in putting the finishing touches to the in-depth media coverage they had painstakingly organised in the wee small hours of that morning.

Gregory had been closely followed by Dr Stillwell, who had yet to tell anyone about his extraordinary win, apart perhaps from one person - name undisclosed? Following swiftly in the Doctor's footsteps came Sessile and Linda and indeed, by ten o'clock, more or less all the Committee members were seated for the definitive meeting - bar one.

"I would like to make this as short as possible," began Miss Ploughman as she stood up from her chair facing the Committee members, "because we all have a number of things to do today. But without your help, and the undying hunger for success you have shown throughout this voyage in uncharted waters, this project quite possibly would never have come into being, or accomplished so seamlessly. I am enormously grateful for your anchor of support, and forever in your debt, and judging by the projection that Mrs Bircher has received from the accountant - which no doubt she will pass around in a few moments - I feel for the most part you can be justifiably pleased - to say the very least. With that said . . . ." - and Miss Ploughman bent over to pick up her papers which had been blown to the newly installed, polished teak floor from the matching table by a current of wind from the front doors of the pub, while the Committee members sat waiting, humbled by her words of deep gratitude. "Before that, however," continued Miss Ploughman, "I would like to hand you over to the Major who I know would like to say a few words."

With a warm ripple of applause, Major Shoreshot began to stand, only to hear Melvin pipe up and say, "If you bent over any further you'd eclipse the sun!"

On hearing this shocking outburst of insulting words, Mrs Bircher arose from her chair to say, "Don't be so vulgar, Melvin!" In consequence, Melvin then found it most necessary to retaliate with the obscenity, "Show us your knickers, you old custard tart!"

"Melvin! Stop that!" came a stern and forbidding voice from the front door of The Pieced and Broke Arms, and everyone turned around in full agreement to see that it was Paul, who had just about struggled his way through the double front doors of the pub with the aid of a pair of crutches. Although still in great pain,

Paul was determined to be involved in at least a part of the meeting, and his laboured entrance had caused the blast of hot air that had blown Miss Ploughman's papers to the floor in the first place.

Melvin's reaction on hearing his master's voice was to bury his head in the nineteen remaining feathers on his chest, while lifting his right leg from the perch and swinging it to and fro like a child that has been caught misbehaving.

Rosina was not amongst the gathering as she was roping off the parking areas for the two hefty coaches that would be on their way within the next few hours for the first sitting at five o'clock that afternoon. As anticipated, she had made precise and accurate measurements to accommodate both long vehicles, enabling easy access for passengers to disembark on arrival at the drop off point, and rejoin their allocated coach at the pick-up point after dining. These dividing ropes would then be taken down ready for the next sitting which was reserved for all regional television stations and the full-scale press coverage that Gregory and his sisters had set up, together with complete live broadcast from Douglas and Howard Pratt who would be transmitting their show from inside the pub, under a specially reworked title of Plug Your Own Leak, at the slightly later time of 20.30 hours for one night only. Their arrival was going to be something of a showstopper that no-one would expect, only to commence while the arranged media were taking pre-dinner drinks outside in the exquisitely colourful beer garden. A predetermined time had been set by Gregory and, at 19.35 hours, a hot air balloon in the shape of a bottle emblazoned with a full listing of the beers and the name of the pub would float past at a height of one hundred and twenty feet; whereupon Douglas and Howard Pratt would descend the first eighty feet by rope ladder, then drop into freefall for the remaining forty feet straight into the net at the entrance of the Eager Beaver Trail. In the unlikely event of there being a catastrophe, both Pratts would be wearing their extra padded fancy dress plum suits for additional, hopefully-not-needed protection!

Unbeknown to Gregory, Tiberius had also made arrangements for a surprise visit of a not so dissimilar nature, having spoken secretly and privately with Humphrey, an old pilot friend, who owned a number of classic aircraft in pristine condition and full working order from the Second World War - a most desirable collection to have. Only after a tremendous amount of pleading, Tiberius had managed to persuade Humphrey to bring these magnificent and finely crafted pieces of airborne art out of retirement and back to their rightful home - a place where they truly belonged - the sky. The two 1944 Hurricanes would approach from the east, while at the same time the 1943 Spitfire would approach from the west and fly in between the two oncoming Hurricanes while doing a victory roll .... at an altitude of one hundred and twenty feet .... at 19.35 hours!

An intense conversation was underway between Nigel and Miss Ploughman, owing to the fact that Nigel had made a full recovery the day before from his most recent encounter with his visually obvious affliction, Knocking Knee Syndrome. Nigel, it must be said, somehow now looked better than ever before .... in fact, Miss Ploughman truly had to look twice to recognise him. "You're planning to do what?" said Miss Ploughman to Nigel.

"Yes, you heard right. I'm going to fly over The Pieced and Broke Arms at 19.35 hours. Having catapulted myself from the end of the Eager Beaver Trail, and on reaching the desired height of one hundred and twenty feet, I will engage my motorised parachute and attempt a barrel roll over the top of the Pub," said Nigel.

"Well…. I do know that Gregory has also got something planned, although he declined to tell me exactly what that would be," said Miss Ploughman. She had assumed, of course, that Nigel must have been joking and, in that belief, added a slightly supercilious remark: "Alright, Nigel. Whatever takes your fancy!"

…. To be continued. …

About the Author

R J Neale grew up in the South East of England until the Spring of 1986 when, at the age of twenty one, he moved to Cornwall with his family. Now engaged jointly with his brother in managing a successful business in the city of Truro, he has recently turned his hand to creative writing. A Summer Talent is the first novel to be published from his forthcoming trilogy.

Printed in the United Kingdom
by Lightning Source UK Ltd.
128150UK00002B/73-357/P